Hello, friend!

Rebecca Cobb

MACMILLAN CHILDREN'S BOOKS

I love to play with my friend.

We play
all sorts
of things.

We love to
jump around,

and go fast
on the bike.

I show my friend how to build
tall towers. He's doing very well.

I'm really good at sharing . . .

especially at lunchtimes.

And I'm extra helpful when we put our coats on.

We're so excited to go outside!

We would stay out all
day long if we could.

Sometimes we
do quiet things,

and sometimes we do noisy things.

Other times we do nothing at all.

I'm always sad when it's time to go home,

because I will miss my friend.

I hope he misses me?

I think he might!

And even though I don't like
to say goodbye, I can't wait
until tomorrow . . .

because I'm looking forward
to all the fun we can have . . .

together.

I really love to play with my friend,
and my friend loves to play with me.

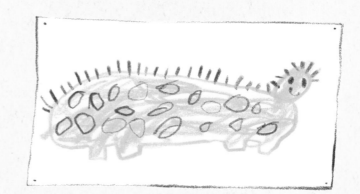